THE ENORMOUS POTATO

To my mother, Edith Cohen. – A.D.

In memory of my mother and father, who first told me this tale many years ago. – D.P.

First U.S. edition 1998

Text copyright © 1997 by Aubrey Davis
Illustrations and hand lettering copyright © 1997 by Dušan Petričić

Kids Can Press Ltd. acknowledges with appreciation the assistance of the Canada Council and the Ontario Arts Council in the production of this book.

Published in Canada by: Published in the U.S. by:
Kids Can Press Ltd.   Kids Can Press Ltd.
29 Birch Avenue   85 River Rock Drive, Suite 202
Toronto, ON M4V 1E2   Buffalo, NY 14207

The artwork in this book was rendered in watercolor and pencil on 140 lb Bockingford watercolor paper.
Text is set in Bodoni

Edited by Debbie Rogosin and Trudee Romanek
Printed in Hong Kong by Wing King Tong Co. Ltd.

97 0 9 8 7 6 5 4 3 2 1

Canadian Cataloguing in Publication Data

Davis, Aubrey
    The enormous potato

ISBN 1-55074-386-4

I. Petricic, Dusan. II. Title.

PS8557.A832E56   1997   jC813'.54   C97-930196-3
PZ7.D38En   1997

THE

RETOLD BY
AUBREY DAVIS

ENORMOUS
POTATO

ILLUSTRATED BY **DUŠAN PETRIČIĆ**

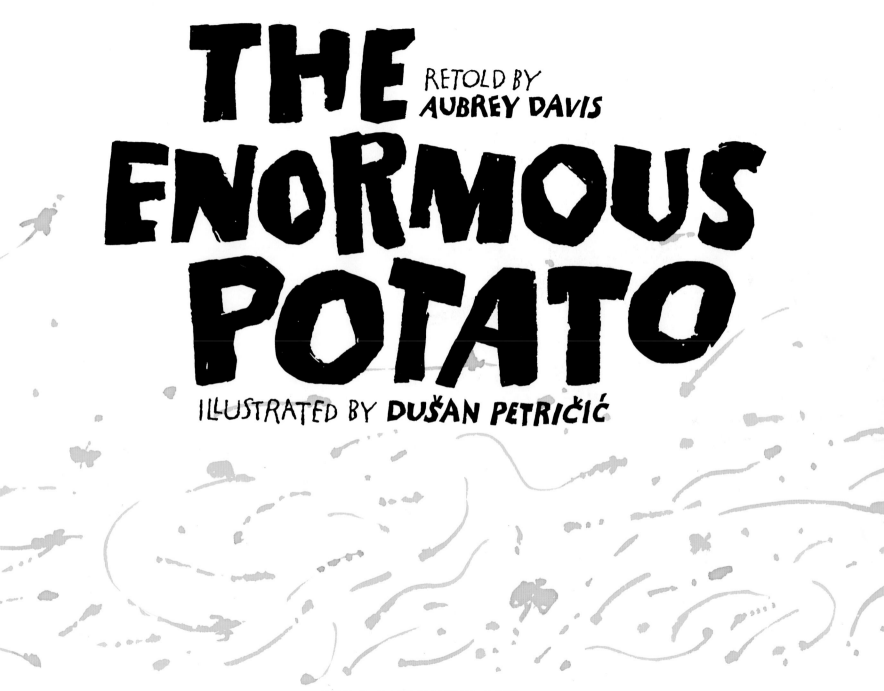

KIDS CAN PRESS LTD.

There once was a farmer who had an eye.
It wasn't like your eye or my eye.
It was a potato eye.
The farmer planted it.
And it grew into a potato.

The potato grew bigger and bigger.

It grew fat.
It grew enormous.

It was the biggest potato
in the world.

"It's time to pull it out,"
said the farmer.
So he grabbed the potato.
He pulled and pulled again.
But the potato wouldn't
come out of the ground.
So he called his wife.

The wife grabbed the farmer.
The farmer grabbed the potato.
They pulled and pulled again.
But the potato wouldn't
come out of the ground.
So the wife called their daughter.

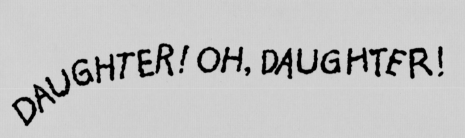

The daughter grabbed the wife.
The wife grabbed the farmer.
The farmer grabbed the potato.
They pulled and pulled again.
But the potato wouldn't
come out of the ground.
So the daughter called the dog.

"ROWF! ROWF! ROWF!"

The dog grabbed the daughter.
The daughter grabbed the wife.
The wife grabbed the farmer.
The farmer grabbed the potato.
They pulled and pulled again.
But the potato wouldn't
come out of the ground.
So the dog called the cat.

"MEOW! MEOW! MEOW!"

The cat grabbed the dog.

The dog grabbed the daughter.

The daughter grabbed the wife.

The wife grabbed the farmer.

The farmer grabbed the potato.

They pulled and pulled again.

But the potato wouldn't
come out of the ground.

So the cat called the mouse.

"SQUEAK! SQUEAK! SQUEAK!"

The mouse grabbed the cat.

The cat grabbed the dog.

The dog grabbed the daughter.

The daughter grabbed the wife.

The wife grabbed the farmer.

The farmer grabbed the potato.

They pulled and pulled again.

RRRRRRRRRRRRRRRRRRRRRRRRRRRR...RIP!

Out came the potato!

"That's a big potato!"
said the farmer.
"That's a big potato!"
said the wife.
"That's a dirty potato!"
said the daughter.
So they washed it,
    and chopped it,
        and cooked it, too.

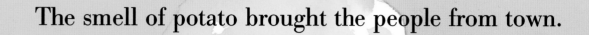
The smell of potato brought the people from town.

They brought forks.

They brought bowls.

They brought butter and salt.

Soon everyone was eating potato.

My, it was good.

They ate and they ate . . .

till the potato was gone.

And now the story is gone, too.